Malcolm often plays the butter[...] is a little bit silly and not very [...] but I don't think that's very fa[...] After all, a butterfly probably *would* expect all babies to look very different from their parents.

Did you know?

Monkeys have unique fingerprints, just like humans!

As well as performing the story, it's good fun singing the *Monkey Puzzle* song. After I wrote the lyrics, I learned them in Makaton so that I could sign it too. You can watch me singing the song and doing the actions on the Gruffalo website, Gruffalo.com. Why don't you have a go, too?

And now, with Butterfly's help, little monkey has been looking for – and finding – his mum for 20 years. So I'd like to wish them all a very happy birthday!

Julia Donaldson

What do you think?

Butterflies aren't the only animals that don't look like their children.

Can you think of any others?

For Tommy, Billy, Emma and Katie – J.D.

First published 2000 by Macmillan Children's Books
This edition published 2020 by Macmillan Children's Books
an imprint of Pan Macmillan
The Smithson, 6 Briset Street, London EC1M 5NR
Associated companies throughout the world
www.panmacmillan.com

ISBN: 978-1-5290-2778-5

1 3 5 7 9 8 6 4 2

A CIP catalogue record for this book is available from the British Library.

Printed in China.

WRITTEN BY
JULIA DONALDSON

ILLUSTRATED BY
AXEL SCHEFFLER

Monkey Puzzle

MACMILLAN CHILDREN'S BOOKS

"I've lost my mum!"

"Hush, little monkey, don't you cry.
I'll help you find her," said Butterfly.
"Let's have a think. How big is she?"

"She's big!" said the monkey. "Bigger than me."

"Bigger than you? Then I've seen your mum.
Come, little monkey, come, come, come."

"No, no, no! That's an elephant.

"My mum isn't a great grey hunk.
She hasn't got tusks or a curly trunk.
She doesn't have great thick baggy knees.
And anyway, *her* tail coils round trees."

"She coils round trees? Then she's very near.
Quick, little monkey! She's over here."

"No, no, no! That's a snake.

"Mum doesn't look a *bit* like this.
She doesn't slither about and hiss.
She doesn't curl round a nest of eggs.
And anyway, my mum's got more legs."

"It's legs *we're* looking for now, you say?
I know where she is, then. Come this way."

"No, no, no! That's a spider.

"Mum isn't black and hairy and fat.
She's not got so many legs as *that!*
She'd rather eat fruit than swallow a fly,
And she lives in the treetops, way up high."

"She lives in the trees? You should have said!

Your mummy's hiding above your head."

"No, no, no! That's a parrot.

"Mum's got a nose and not a beak.
She doesn't squawk and squabble and shriek.
She doesn't have claws or feathery wings.
And anyway, my mum leaps and springs."

"Aha! I've got it! She leaps about?
She's just round the corner, without a doubt."

"No, no, no! That's a frog!

"Butterfly, butterfly, please don't joke!
Mum's not green and she doesn't croak.
She's not all slimy. Oh dear, what a muddle!
She's brown and furry, and nice to cuddle."

"Brown fur – why didn't you tell me so?
We'll find her in no time – off we go!"

"No, no, no! That's a bat.

"Why do you keep on getting it wrong?
Mum doesn't sleep the whole day long.
I told you, she's got no wings at all,
And anyway, she's not *nearly* so small!"

"Your mum's not little? Now let me think.

She's down by the river, having a drink!"

"NO, NO, NO!
That's the elephant again!

"Butterfly, butterfly, can't you see?
None of these creatures looks like me!"

"You never told me she looked like you!"

"Of course I didn't! I thought you knew!"

"I didn't know. I couldn't! You see . . .

". . . None of my babies looks like me.
So she looks like you! Well, if that's the case
We'll soon discover her hiding place."

"No, no, no! That's my dad!"

"Come, little monkey, come, come, come.
It's time I took you home to . . ."

"Mum!"

Illustrator Axel Scheffler drew lots of different monkeys in his sketchbook to work out how the little monkey should look. Here are some of his drawings. Do any of them look similar to the little monkey who appears in the finished story?

Axel tried lots of different versions for the butterfly, too. He eventually decided on the bright blue butterfly you can see in the book.

Did you know?

Butterflies often have brightly coloured wings which are a warning to other animals that they are not good to eat!